PRICE STERN SLOAN
Published by the Penguin Group
Penguin Group (USA) LLC, 375 Hudson Street, New York, New York 10014, USA

USA | Canada | UK | Ireland | Australia | New Zealand | India | South Africa | China

penguin.com
A Penguin Random House Company

Published in 2014 by Price Stern Sloan, a division of
Penguin Young Readers Group, 345 Hudson Street, New York, New York 10014.
PSS! is a registered trademark of Penguin Group (USA) LLC.
Printed in the USA.

ISBN 978-0-8431-8105-0   10 9 8 7 6 5 4 3 2 1

INTRODUCTION

Principal Brown asked me to discuss the rules of Elmore Junior High with you.

When it comes to running a disciplined and orderly school—which I have done for many thousands of years—it is important for everyone to be disciplined and orderly.

Many of you think it's okay to run around here willy-nilly like wild animals, but—

Miss Simian, we *are* wild animals. I'm a cat. Darwin here is a fish. Tina is a T. rex. Not to mention all the fruits, vegetables, and living peanuts with antlers in the student body. Even *you're* a baboon.

I'm a *whaaaaat?*

Maybe you should just let her talk about her willies and her nillies, Gumball.
What does "willy-nilly" even mean?
Keep your thoughts to yourself, Gumball. That will be one white card for you.
What's a white card?
A white card means you're in deep trouble.
Now, as I was saying before I got so rudely interrupted, we are here to discuss the rules of Elmore Junior High.
Take detailed notes, as there will be nine pop quizzes, several oral tests, and three final exams on this material tomorrow.
Oh man . . .
Gumball, stop interrupting! That makes two more white cards for you!

CONTENTS

SECTION 1

GENERAL

RULES

UNEXCUSED ABSENCES

Anyone caught engaging in truancy, unauthorized tardiness, or cutting classes will be subject to disciplinary action.

What does "truancy" mean, Darwin?

It means staying out of school for no good reason.

There's always a good reason for staying out of school.

Really?

Sure. There's video games, visiting the zoo, sitting on the porch, practicing kung fu, sleeping, watching squirrels, counting blue cars that drive past your house, eating peanut butter without worrying about someone having an allergic attack—

Gumball, maybe you should quit while you're ahead.

But I'm on a roll, Darwin, old pal. There's also watching grass grow, daytime court reality shows, amusement parks, lining up sticks to spell messages for low-flying UFOs, waiting for the mailman to bring your next issue of *Kitty Litter Monthly* . . .

DID I MENTION THE RULE ABOUT SAYING IDIOTIC THINGS IN SCHOOL? YOU'VE JUST EARNED YOURSELF ANOTHER WHITE CARD!

ABSENCES

Any absence requires a note from a parent or guardian. Forging a note will result in your parent or guardian being notified.

Help Gumball forge a note to Principal Brown.

DEAR PRINCIPAL NIGEL .... BROWN,
                          FUNNY NICKNAME

PLEASE EXCUSE OUR .... SON, GUMBALL, FROM SCHOOL.
                        ADJECTIVE

HE HAS AN URGENT APPOINTMENT WITH HIS .... TODAY.
                                            A PROFESSION

HE INJURED HIS .... WHILE HELPING A/AN .... LADY
                  BODY PART   *ADJECTIVE*

CROSS THE STREET WHILE HE WAS ON HIS WAY TO VOLUNTEER

TO .... THE HOMELESS. THIS BOY IS ....
       VERB   *ADVERB*

AMAZING. EVEN THOUGH HE WAS INJURED, HE STILL STOPPED

TO HELP A/AN .... GET OUT OF A/AN ....
                  ANIMAL   *NOUN*

VERY TRULY YOURS,

Nicole Watterson (GUMBALL'S MOM)

PS: PLEASE EXCUSE MY .... HANDWRITING.
                          ADJECTIVE

I INJURED MY .... WHILE PLAYING ....
                BODY PART   *A WEIRD SPORT*

FIGHTING

Elmore Junior High has a zero-tolerance policy for roughhousing on school property.

ELECTRONIC DEVICES

Radios, MP3 players, cell phones, and all other electronic devices not being used for instructional purposes must be left in your locker at all times.

Help Juke identify his classmates and teachers by spotting parts of them through holes in his locker.

1 It's ....!

2 It's ....!

3 It's ....!

4 It's ....!

5 It's ....!

6 It's ....!

7 It's ....!

8 It's ....!

9 It's ....!

10 It's ....!

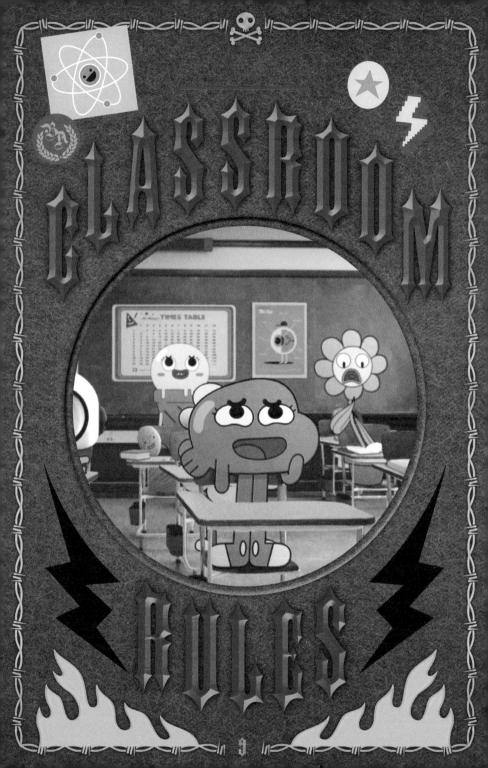

BE PROMPT

Arrive at class on time or a little early.
Rushing in while the bell is ringing
will constitute a tardy.

I don't like being tardy, Gumball. Everyone stares at you while you walk to your seat. Plus, the teacher gives you a white card.

Getting a white card is a badge of honor, Darwin. I'm not athletic. I'm not supersmart. I don't have money oozing from my pores. However, getting white cards is something I'm good at.

And what does that get you?

Principal Brown told me five white cards get you a yellow card. Five yellow cards get you a red card. Five red cards get you a silver card. Guess what five silver cards get you?

Suspended?

No, five silver cards get you a gold card. Only one kid in the history of Elmore Junior High has ever gotten one. Rumor has it that there's a platinum diamond carbonite card after that. It's my life's goal to find out.

Five white cards get you a yellow card.

Five yellow cards get you a red card.

Five red cards get you a silver card.

Five silver cards get you a gold card.

So how many white cards does it take to get a gold card?

A.   125

B.   400

C.   500

D.   625

RESPECT

Always refer to your teacher by his or her title and last name.

CLASSROOM PROTOCOL

Raise your hand when you want to ask a question or make a comment.

Miss Simian—

Darwin, you must raise your hand if you wish to speak.

I told you to raise your hand, Darwin. That's five white cards and a detention for Gumball!

What?!?

But, Miss Simian—

You were going to make some smart-aleck comment, so I figured I'd beat you to the punch.

But, Miss Simian, Tina stepped on Banana Joe. His banana goop is squishing out all over the floor!

Darwin, I told you to RAISE YOUR HAND!!! That's another white card for Gumball. On your way to Principal Brown's office, please ask Robbie the janitor to come down here with his mop and squeegee.

Build your official title using the key below.

1 First letter of your first name: ☐

   A through E: **ADMIRAL**
   F through J: **BARON/BARONESS**
   K through O: **COUNT/COUNTESS**
   P through T: **DUKE/DUCHESS**
   U through Z: **EMPEROR/EMPRESS**

2 Last letter of your first name: ☐

   A through E: **FIDALGO**
   F through J: **GUARDIAN IMMORTAL**
   K through O: **HERZOG**
   P through T: **IMRAN**
   U through Z: **JAGIRDAR**

3 First letter of your last name: ☐

   A through E: **KUMAR**
   F through J: **LONKO**
   K through O: **MAYOR OF AWESOMEVILLE**
   P through T: **NATIONAL SECURITY ADVISOR**
   U through Z: **OVERLORD**

4 Month of your birth: ☐

   January/February: **COMMISSIONER OF KICKBALL**
   March/April: **PRIME MINISTER**
   May/June: **QUEEN/KING**
   July/August: **ROJU**
   September/October: **WONTON SOUP MASTER**
   November/December: **SERGEANT**

5 **Insert your first name:**

6 **Favorite color:**

Red: **BOISTEROUS**
Orange: **ULTIMATE GUARDIAN**
Yellow: **CHARMINGEST**
Green: **YOUR HIGHNESS**
Blue: **HAMMER**
Purple: **FIRE MARSHAL**
Pink: **RAINBOW UNICORN**
Clear: **VAPID**

7 **Insert your last name:**

8 **Your age:**

5 and under = **THE PEAPOD**
6 = **THE SIXTH**
7 = **THE SEVENTH**
8 = **THE EIGHTH**
9 = **THE NINTH**
10 = **THE TENTH**
11 = **THE ELEVENTH**
12 = **THE TWELFTH**
13 and up = **THE ELDERLY**

Your title:

MISSED WORK

If you expect to be away from school because of an emergency, tell your teacher in advance and ask for any work you will miss.

When I'm absent, I *never* miss my work.

What do you mean, Gumball? You missed four assignments last week alone!

No, Darwin, my fishy friend, I neglected to do them, but I did not *miss* them one bit!

When I'm absent, I ask Anais to bring my assignments home for me. She's very responsible.

You should ask Alan to bring your assignments to you. He has no hands, so you'd have an excuse for when you don't get your work done.

I'd be happy to help you out, Darwin!

FOOD

Do not chew gum or eat candy or other food in class unless you have been given special permission.

Miss Simian, does this rule apply to any sort of gum?

Of course it does, Darwin.

And you're sure Tina has been given special permission?

There are no exceptions to this rule.

Then if Gumball gets special permission, can he get out of Tina's mouth?

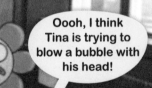

Oooh, I think Tina is trying to blow a bubble with his head!

Help Gumball wiggle his way out of another missed assignment by writing in his excuses!

Gumball, where is your homework?

I don't believe that for a second!

Please, Gumball, do you think I was born yesterday?!?

Well, that's not completely unbelievable. Tell me more.

Okay, you have a one-day extension on the project.

All right, you're excused entirely, but not until you bring this love note—ahem, *attendance report* to Principal Brown.

CHEATING

**Never cheat on a test.
Both the student who shares his work AND the person who copies it will receive a zero.**

PASSING NOTES

Passing notes is strictly prohibited.

Find all the hidden words. Put the uncircled letters together to discover Gumball's secret message.

HIDDEN WORDS: ANAIS, BANANA JOE, BOOM BOX, DARWIN, FINS, FISH, FUNNY, FURRY, GUMBALL, HOT DOG GUY, MISS SIMIAN, PENNY, RAINBOW, TOAST, WATTERSON.

Y	O	G	U	M	B	A	L	L	M
U	W	B	H	R	B	R	E	R	I
A	B	A	O	T	H	S	T	A	S
F	O	N	T	I	A	N	A	I	S
U	O	A	D	T	P	F	I	N	S
N	M	N	O	O	E	U	F	B	I
N	B	A	G	A	N	R	I	O	M
Y	O	J	G	S	N	R	S	W	I
N	X	O	U	T	Y	Y	H	O	A
K	S	E	Y	D	A	R	W	I	N

GOING OUTSIDE

When your class is called, quietly form two lines at the assigned door. Quietly walk down the hall to your locker to collect your coat if needed. Then line up at the assigned door to be led out for recess.

Is this recess or basic training?

I think they both have the same goal. We have recess because federal guidelines require kids to get a certain amount of exercise each week. These requirements can be met through recess, sports activities, gym class, or a combination of the three.

So, Darwin, how's your neck been feeling?

My neck? It's fine. Why?

It must be sore from carrying around your giant brain all the time.

BASIC RULES

NO RUNNING ON
THE BLACKTOP.

NO CLIMBING UP THE SLIDE.

NO JUMPING
OFF THE SWINGS.

DO NOT JUMP FROM THE TOP
OF THE CLIMBING WALL.

NO SKATEBOARDING.

NO EATING OR GUM-CHEWING.

NO TACKLING, PUNCHING,
OR ROUGHHOUSING.

Wow, there are more rules for being outside school than for being inside!
That's because more kids get hurt on the playground than anyplace else at school. They're concerned about the liability.
Does *liability* mean that kids should have a totally boring life and look back at their childhood with sadness and regret?
No, *liability* means the school is responsible for our well-being. They can get in trouble if we get hurt.
My brain hurts from listening to Miss Simian blabber all day. Who has liability for that?

SAFE DISTANCES

No running within ten feet of any playground equipment.

Help Gumball run from one side of the playground to the other while avoiding Principal Brown and Miss Simian.

START

FINISH

KICKBALL

Play on the grass only. Do not kick balls
on or near playground equipment.

Hey Darwin, I've just invented a new game. It's called mega-extreme super kickball.

Ooh, how do you play?

It's the same as regular kickball, but you play it in the middle of the playground equipment.

TETHERBALL

No holding the ball or rope during play.
No stepping on the other player's side
of the circle. If these rules are
broken, the player is out.

I'm beginning to feel like this is more like a jail yard than a playground.

What do you mean, Gumball?

All these rules. It's hard to keep track of them all! Plus that tetherball over there . . . It looks like a ball and chain!

Oh, you're just imagining things.

CHILDREN, WE WILL BE ASKING EVERYONE TO START WEARING ORANGE JUMPSUITS AND ANKLE SHACKLES AT RECESS.

THE SWINGS

Students are not allowed to jump off, twist,
or stand on swings. Classmates are not allowed
to push each other. Swings must be shared.
Everyone is allowed approximately
four minutes per turn.

If I only get four minutes and no one can push me, how will I ever achieve my life's goal?

What's your life's goal, Gumball?

I want to swing so high that I spin all the way around.

That's impossible.

Napoleon said, "*Impossible* is a word to be found only in the dictionary of fools."

And how did things turn out for Napoleon?

Great. He had a nifty hat and a cool uniform.

COMING INSIDE

Students should not bring anything back into school that they find outside on the playground, such as animals or bugs, sticks, wood chips, snow, ice, etc.

What are you doing, Gumball?

I'm blowing all the air out of my lungs.

Why are you doing that?

I breathed in the air on the playground, and I'm not allowed to bring it inside.

What's that banging noise?

I locked everyone else outside. With all the gravel on people's shoes, dirt on their hands, and wood chips stuck to their pant legs, you can never be too sure.

GUMBALL, THAT WILL BE TWENTY-SEVEN WHITE CARDS AND A VISIT TO PRINCIPAL BROWN'S OFFICE FOR YOU. PLEASE BRING HIM THIS BOX, WHICH IS NOT FILLED WITH AN ANNIVERSARY GIFT OF A DOZEN CHOCOLATE-COVERED STRAWBERRIES.

CAFETERIA
RULES

PATIENCE

Students must be patient while waiting to be served. A single-file line must be maintained.

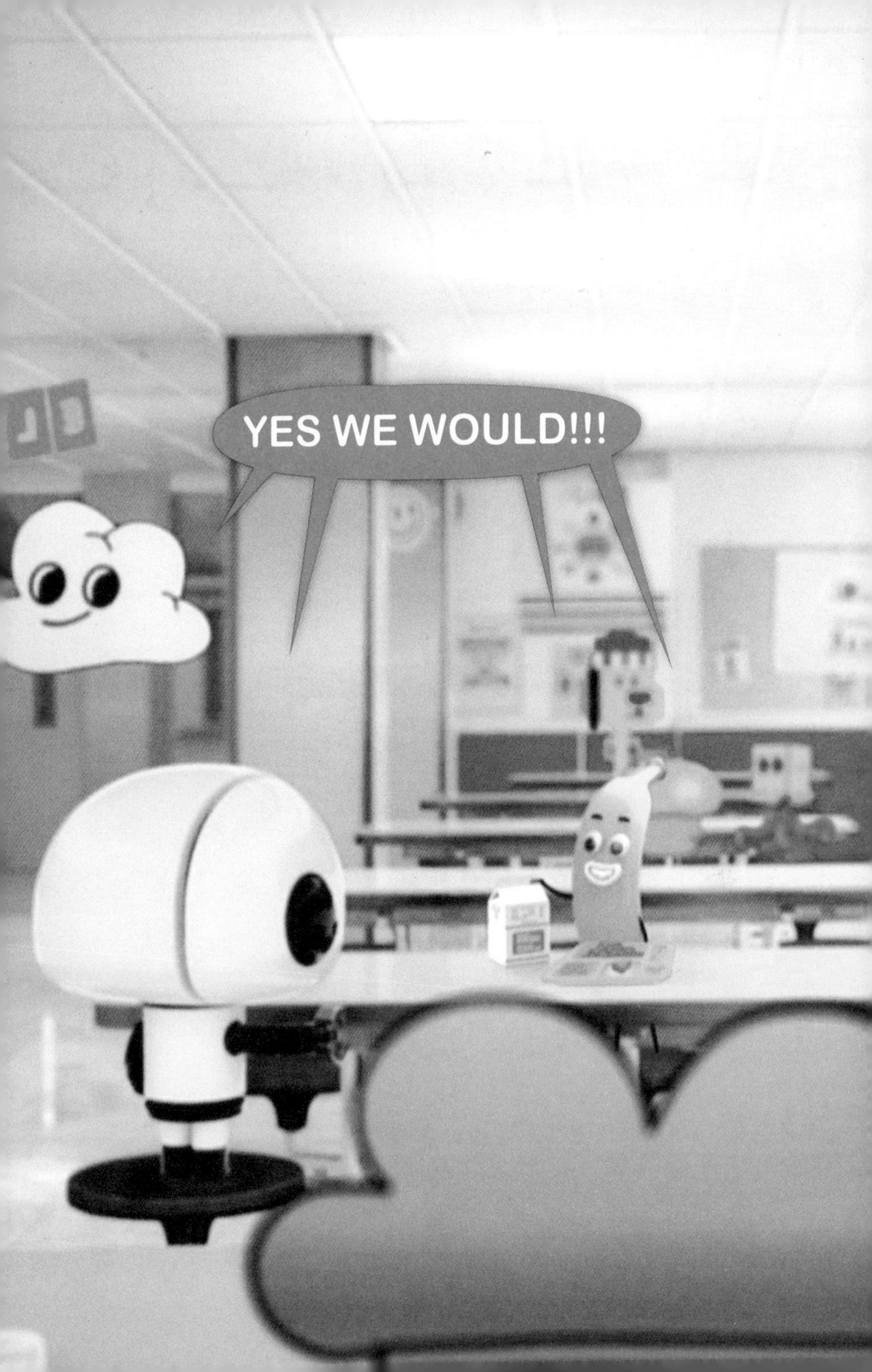
YES WE WOULD!!!

CUTTING

There will be no cutting in line.

I didn't cut Darwin in line, Miss Simian. I *budged* him. There's no rule against that.

Gumball! The rule clearly states there will be no cutting in line.

Oh . . . Okay . . . But I've got both my eyes on both of you!

Dude, that was amazing. Where did you find *that* word?

There's also jumping, butting, barging, budding, skipping, ditching, breaking, shorting, and pushing in. I found it in this book I discovered. It's called a thesaurus.

What's a thesaurus?

I don't know . . . This book doesn't list any synonyms for it.

RESPECT

Treat lunch servers with the same respect
you would show your teachers.

SEATING

Choose a seat and remain in that seat. You must raise your hand and receive permission to move.

MANNERS

Use good table manners at all times.

Did you know?

Did you know that in Thailand it's rude to point the soles of your feet to someone?

No problem then for Leslie, since he's a flower and has roots instead of feet.

And in Greece, it's considered bad manners to show your open palm to anyone.

I wonder if they're offended by open paws . . .

In Kuwait, you should never pass food with your left hand.

Why would I be passing food, anyway? I'm not sharing food with anyone!

And in the Philippines, never squeeze someone's hand when you shake it.

Why would I want to do that, anyway . . . ?

And chewing gum in public is frowned upon in France.

Well, I guess I'm crossing France off my "places to visit" list!

In Korea, never tip your waiter.

The only tip I have is to STAY AWAY FROM MISS SIMIAN!

FOOD FIGHTS

No throwing or spitting food.

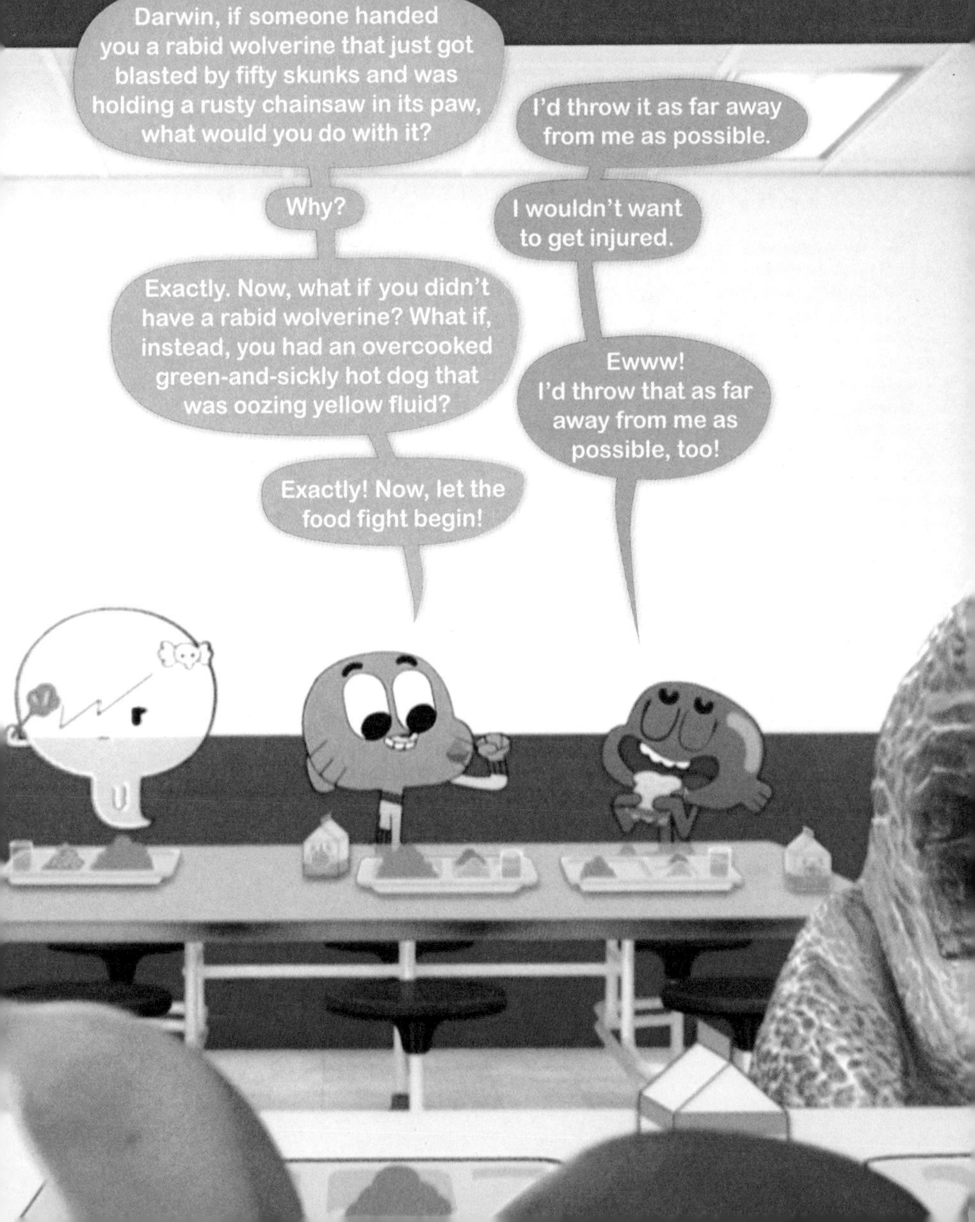

Spot the differences.

CAN YOU SPOT THE FIVE DIFFERENCES BETWEEN THE TWO PICTURES?

TRASH

Tables are to be left neat and cleared of food.
Each table is responsible for this as a group.

Class, has anyone seen Banana Joe, Anton, Idaho, or the Eggheads? They were here before lunch.

My heightened baboon senses tell me someone here knows something about their whereabouts. A white card for each of you if someone doesn't tell me.

Gumball said all food must be cleared from the table. He put them in the trash can!

I did no such thing! I asked them politely to *step into* the garbage can. It's not my fault if they listened.

Gumball, that's fifty white cards for you!

BUS

EMERGENCY EXIT

RULES

GETTING IN

Board the bus promptly in a single-file line;
no shoving or pushing.

Getting the right seat on the bus is very important.

What do you mean?

Sitting in the front means you're a dork. Sitting in the back means you're an outcast. Sitting in the middle means you have no conviction.

Sitting on the right means you're a busybody. Sitting on the left means you're confused—

Sitting by the window means you're antisocial.

Sitting in the middle means you're touchy. Sitting on the aisle means you're nosy—

So, where do we sit??

I . . . DON'T . . . KNOW!!!

ARMS IN

Do not put your arms, hands, head
or feet out the window . . . ever.

_____

What happened to you, Banana Joe?

Mmmfmmffnnmff.

We can't understand you with all those bandages over your mouth.

Mmfmmfmmnnfmrrmdmrr!!

Just because we told you to put your pinkie out the window didn't mean you had to listen to us.

MMFHGHMMMHHGHHDHHGFF!!!!

How rude!

BEHAVIOR

Behave appropriately, just as
if you were in a classroom.

Please refer to the rules
of the cafeteria for my
thoughts on this one . . .

GUMBALL, THAT'S
NINETEEN MORE WHITE
CARDS FOR YOU!

RADIOS

All music must be played through headphones.

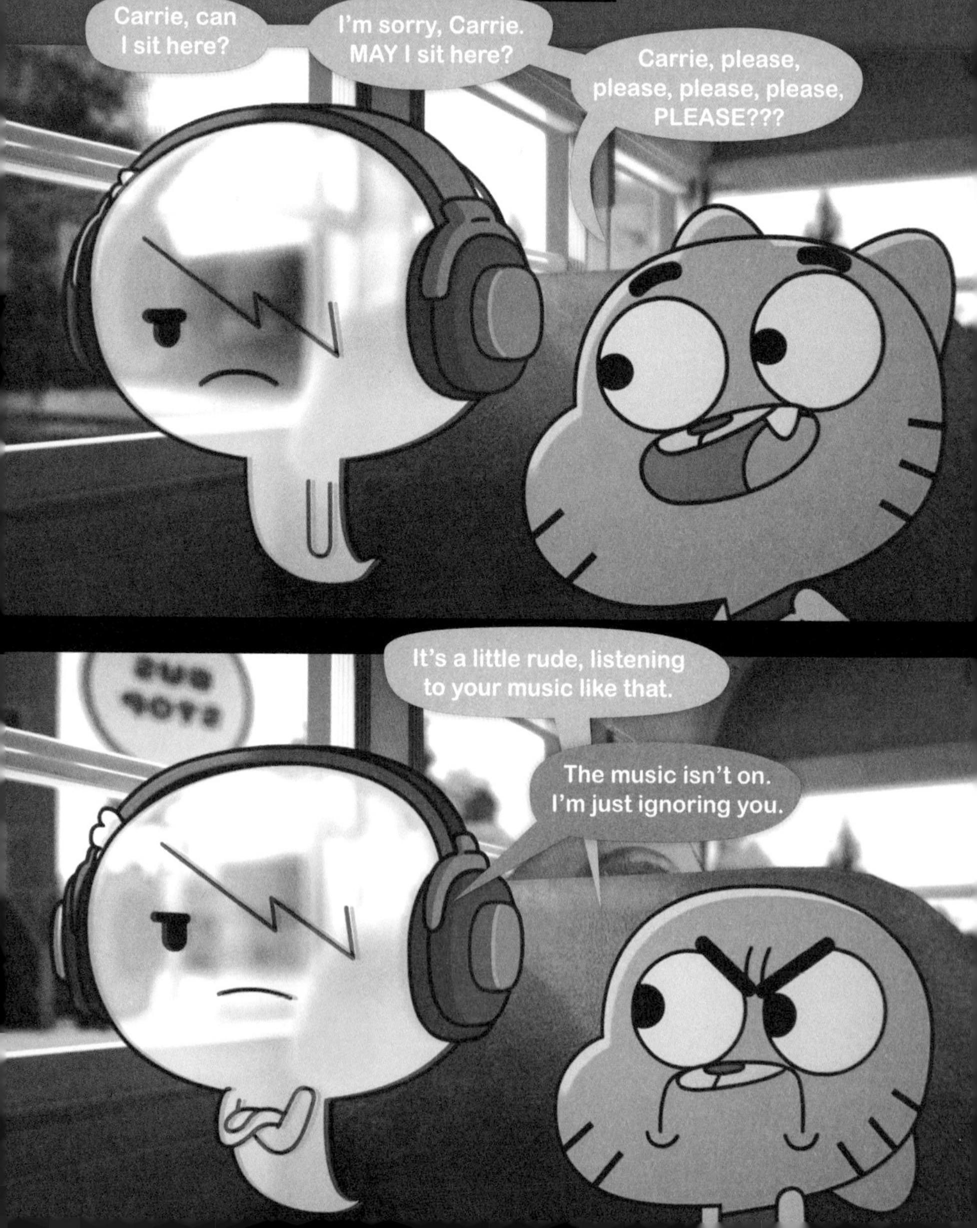

SEATING

Do not damage or deface any part of the bus.

Bus Seat Dot-to-Dot

HELP GUMBALL CONNECT THE DOTS OF INK, SPITBALLS, AND CHEWED GUM TO MAKE A PICTURE OF HIS ARCHENEMY.

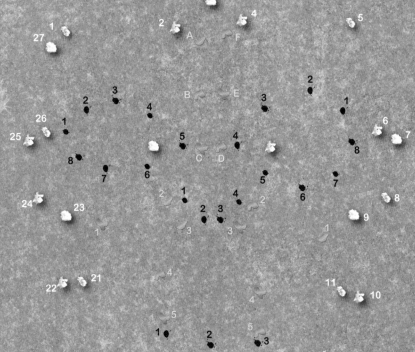

AISLE

Keep the aisle and emergency door clear of obstructions. Books or bags are tripping hazards and can block the way in an emergency.

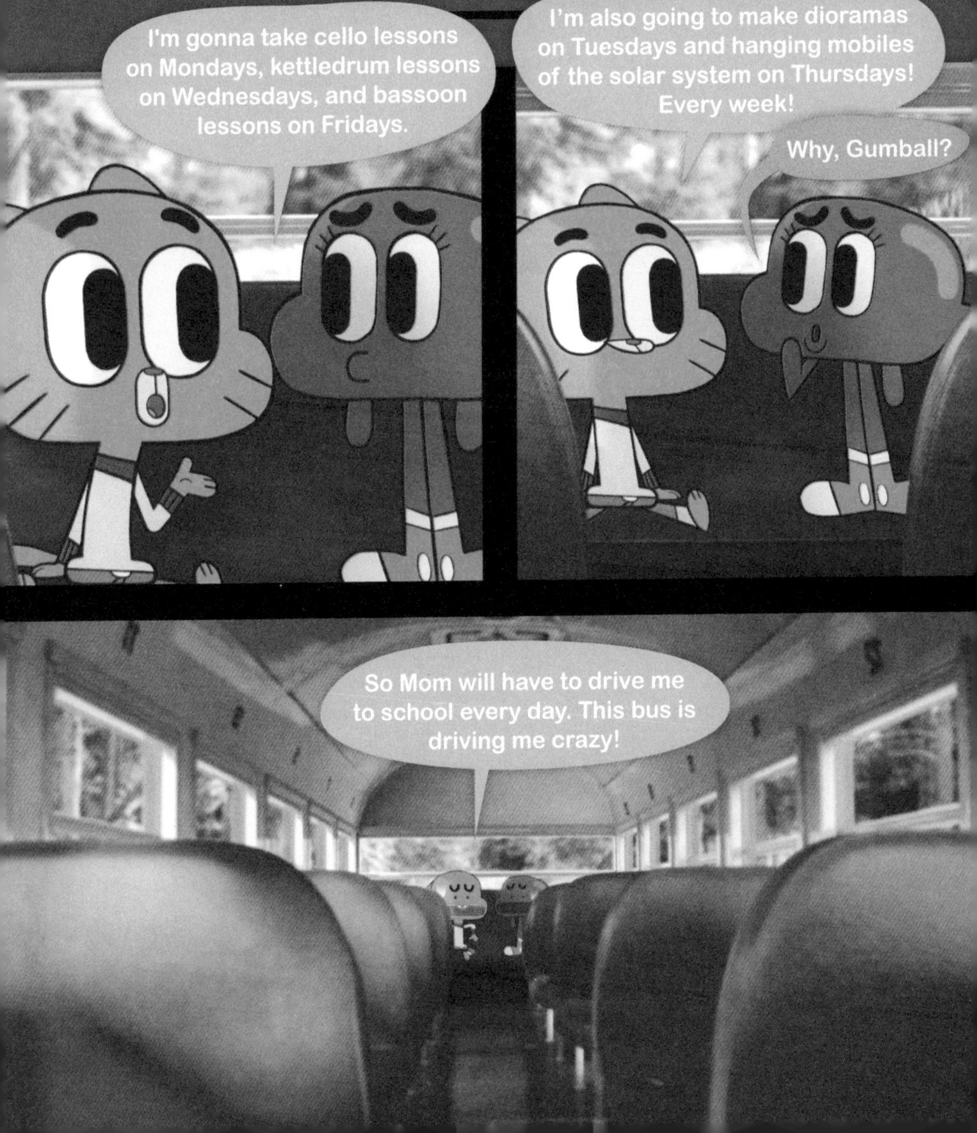

DRESS-CODE
RULES

SHORTS AND SKIRTS

Skirts and shorts must extend below your fingertips when arms are held at your side.

SHIRTS AND TOPS

Midriff-length tops, tank tops, see-through blouses, and shirts with inappropriate writing or logos **ARE NOT ALLOWED.**

The Many Faces of Leslie

DRAW LESLIE EXPRESSING THE EMOTIONS LISTED.

HAPPY

SAD

ANGRY

SCARED

TIRED

CRAZY

FOOTWEAR

No flip-flops, slippers, and/or bare feet at any time.

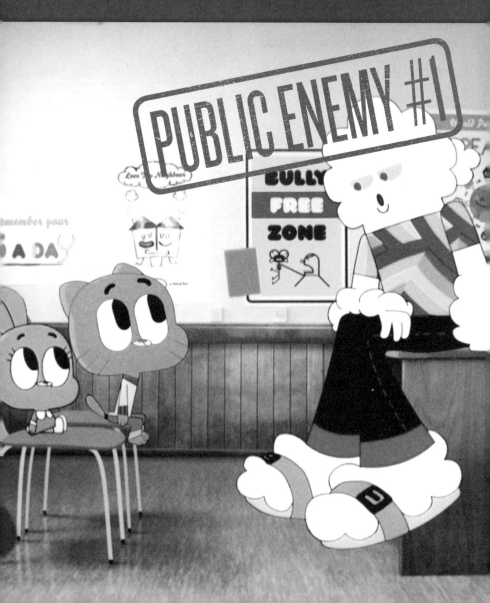

HATS

Hats, hoods, sweatbands, bandannas, sunglasses, goggles, curlers, or headsets are not permitted in the school building.

EMBLEMS

Clothing may not display any images or emblems that may be considered disruptive, distracting, offensive, or upsetting.

EXTRA CREDIT
How many white cards did Gumball earn over the course of this book?

ANSWERS